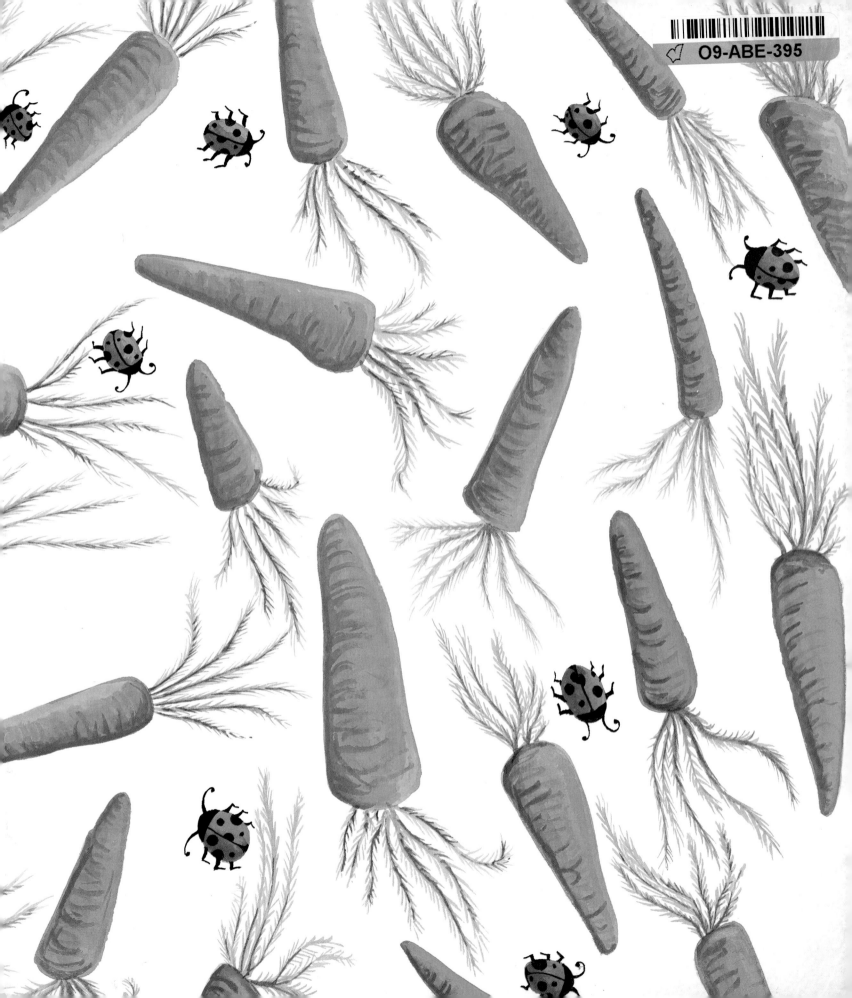

With lots of love to Lindsey Fraser
(who really knows the true worth
of a good blanket)

First American edition 2001 published by Orchard Books
Published simultaneously in Great Britain in 2001 by Orchard Books London

Debi Gliori asserts the right to be identified as the author/illustrator of this work.

Orchard Books, an imprint of Scholastic Inc.
95 Madison Avenue, New York, NY 10016

Manufactured in Dubai
Text design for this edition by Helene Berinsky
The text of this book is set in 31 point Veljovic Medium.
The illustrations are watercolor.

1 3 5 7 9 10 8 6 4 2

Library of Congress Cataloging-in-Publication Data
Gliori, Debi.
Flora's blanket / by Debi Gliori.—lst American ed.
p.   cm.
Summary: Flora, a little rabbit, does not want to sleep without her missing blanket,
so her family helps her look for it.
ISBN 0-531-30305-5 (alk. paper)
[1. Blankets—Fiction. 2. Bedtime—Fiction. 3. Rabbits—Fiction. 4. Lost and found
possessions—Fiction.] I. Title. PZ7.G4889 Fl 2001 [E]—dc21 00-55789

Debi Gliori

Flora's Blanket

Orchard Books • New York

E
GLI

Flora couldn't sleep.

"Poor Flora, what's wrong?"
said her dad. "Sore tummy?"

"No," said Flora.

"Oh, Flora," said her mom.
"Do your ears hurt?"

"No," said Flora.

"Well, what *is* the matter, Flora?"
said her brothers and sisters.

"Why can't you sleep?"

"No blanket,"
said Flora.

"Have mine,"
offered Nora.

"Or mine,"
said Cora.

"No," said Flora.

"Here, take ours,"
said Sam, Tom, and Max.

"No," said Flora.
"Want mine."

"Where is your blanket, Flora?" sighed her mom.

"Don't know," muttered Flora.

"Let's go find it," groaned her dad.

So they looked in
the living room.

"No," said Flora.

And the kitchen.

"No,"
said Flora.

And the bathroom.
"No," said Flora.

Then they looked outside.
The sandbox?

The climbing tree?

The vegetable garden?

"No! NO! NO!"
yelled Flora.

Then they looked
in odd places.
The fridge?

"No,"
sighed
Flora.

The greenhouse?

"No,"
Flora said,
yawning.

The cellar?
"Flora?"
said her dad.

But Flora was
nearly asleep.

Flora's mom and dad tucked her into their bed.

Then they went to bed too.

"What's this lump under my pillow?"
said Flora's dad.

It can't be Flora's teddy bear.

It can't be Flora's book.

It must be . . .

Flora's blanket!

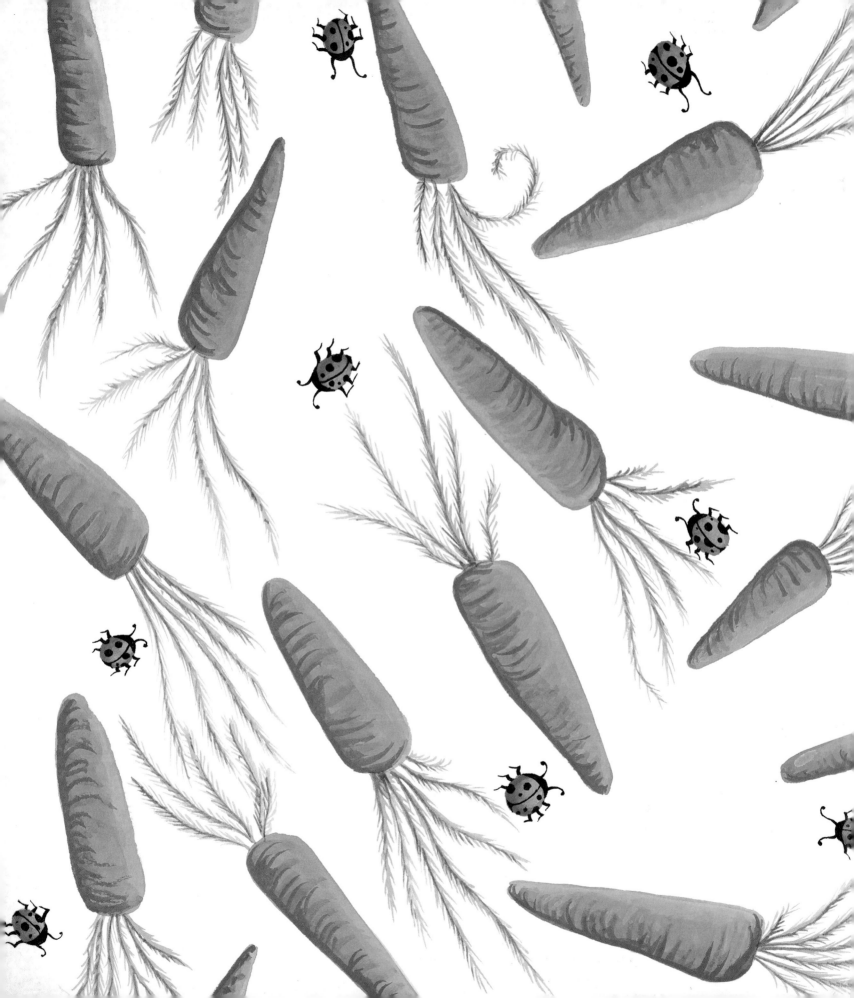